Ramboy

Ramboy

Bethan
Gwanas

*To the pupils of Ysgol y Berwyn, Bala, for helping
me work out the plot in the original Welsh version,
and the pupils of Ysgol y Gader, Dolgellau, for
helping me with teenage-speak in English!*

The publisher acknowledges the support of the
Welsh Books Council

ISBN: 9780862439934

Printed on acid-free and partly recycled paper
and published and bound in Wales by
Y Lolfa Cyf., Talybont, Ceredigion SY24 5HE
e-mail ylolfa@ylolfa.com
website www.ylolfa.com
tel (01970) 832 304
fax 832 782

CHAPTER 1

IT ALL STARTED IN the middle of the night when I woke up feeling really uncomfortable and sweating like mad. I tossed and turned for ages and eventually decided to get up and go to the toilet. It didn't make sense; why was I crawling on all fours along the landing, and why were my pyjama bottoms trailing behind me, hanging off one leg? I should have realised then that something was very wrong, but I was still half asleep, wasn't I?

When I finally made it to the bathroom, I had a few problems getting on to my feet to face the pan. I managed it in the end, but it was all a bit of a mess. It had gone everywhere apart from where it should go. I stared at the puddles on the floor and groaned. Mam was going to kill me. But it was no problem, really: I could blame my dad, or even better, my big brother, Gareth.

Heading for the sink, I had trouble getting to my feet again and had to lean hard on the edge of the sink to see myself in the mirror. That's when I screamed. I was a sheep!

I'm not joking. Honestly, instead of seeing my own face in the mirror – the fairly good looking 13-year-old face of Dewi Lloyd, rugby star of the future – there was a big fat sheep's head staring back at me, a sheep with its mouth wide open and its eyes almost popping out of their sockets. I tried to tell myself it was only a dream. It was just a daft nightmare, that's all, and I'd wake up in a minute. I tried pinching myself – but couldn't. No fingers, no hands, only four stupid, woolly legs which are totally impossible to pinch anything with. This nightmare wasn't much fun. I know they aren't usually that pleasant, that's why they're called nightmares, but this one really sucked. The smell coming off me was just like manky old wool, too.

I trotted back to bed so that I could wake up. Gareth was still grunting and snoring away in the other bed, and he definitely wasn't a sheep. His ugly face was squashed into the pillow, and he was drooling out of the corner of his mouth. He looked more like a bulldog. It was three am on the alarm clock.

Jumping onto my bed, I stuffed my head under the quilt. But within seconds, I was sweating like a pig again (well, a sheep in this case). I kicked the quilt away and just couldn't settle. It's not easy to get comfortable lying on your back when you've got four legs. When was this crazy dream going to end? I was wide awake now, and starving. So I went downstairs to the kitchen (on all fours, head first, which was pretty scary) and opened the fridge door with my nose. It was full, but I didn't really fancy anything, not even the cheese strings, not even the gooey piece of chocolate gâteau that was left over from Sunday.

So I wandered into the living room, which is full of my Mam's precious potted plants, plants she treats with more love and affection than her own children. Before I realised what I was doing, my Mam's Elephant Ear, her favourite plant of all, was in my mouth, down my throat and heading for my stomach.

I stared at the pot: there was nothing left, nothing but a ragged stalk and a bit of compost. It looked awful. But it had tasted so good... really good, wonderfully juicy, the perfect starter. I couldn't resist it; I went round every single plant in the room. I ate every leaf, every flower, every bud. I knew I was being stupid, but I couldn't stop myself.

I felt sleepy after that, so I settled myself on the mat in front of the fireplace, and fell asleep – until I woke up with a start. Beams of sunlight were shooting through the window and I could hear birds singing. I looked at the clock on the mantelpiece: five o'clock. I was stiff, sore and totally naked – where were my pyjamas? Then I realised with a sigh of relief that I had human legs and arms again – I wasn't a sheep! So it must have been a dream after all. I was just getting up with a big grin on my face when I suddenly realised that all my Mam's plants had disappeared. They had been chewed to bits – and oh no, please no... there were sheep droppings all over the carpet, big lumps of black balls absolutely everywhere, and some had been squashed deep into the shag pile. I could feel beads of sweat rising on my forehead, and I started trembling. This nightmare was becoming ridiculous.

I ran upstairs, grabbing my pyjama bottoms from the bathroom floor on the way, and crawled into bed. My head was about to explode and I really didn't think I would be able to fall asleep ever again, but I must have done, because the next thing I heard was: "AAAAAAAAH!"

Mam's voice from the living room below. "My plants! Something has eaten them! Every single one! Every single bit of them! And there are sheep droppings all over my carpet! John! (That's my Dad's name) One of your bloody sheep is in the house! John! Get up! NOW!"

We all had to get up after that. Dad, Gareth, Lowri my nine-year-old sister, and me. Mam sent us all round the house looking for the guilty sheep, but there was no sign of it, obviously.

"I don't get it," said Dad, "is there a window open somewhere?" The only open window was in Lowri's bedroom upstairs, and sheep can't fly. All the doors were shut tight too.

"But what sheep is clever enough to open doors and shut them afterwards?" wailed my mother.

She was really upset and I felt terrible. She was too upset to make us a proper breakfast. We always have a cooked one – she insists that everyone should start the day on a full stomach – but we had to make do with cornflakes. I wasn't very hungry anyway, and I definitely couldn't have faced a plateful of bacon and eggs. The very thought of them made me feel sick.

We had to catch the school bus then, so it was left to my Dad to check the gates and fences around the fields near the house. The others waved at him as the bus pulled away, but I looked away, knowing only too well he wouldn't find a single hole or gap anywhere.

I just couldn't concentrate in class. For one thing, I had a terrible stomach ache. Wind. I managed to let off a few sly ones every now and then, which was quite easy in the chemistry lesson because it always smells funny in there anyway: a permanent whiff of rotten eggs from the magnesium oxide and the sulphur and stuff (and the teacher, come to think of it). But I couldn't get away with it that easily in the other classes, especially French, because the teacher won't let us sit next to our friends, so I always have to sit next to flipping Menna Morgan, who's obsessively clean and tidy and hates my guts. I'm scared to breathe on her, let alone fart next to her. So I managed to keep it in, but my stomach ache was even worse after that. I kept coming out in a cold sweat as well, remembering what I'd done to Mam's poor plants – and the carpet.

I suppose it was the plants' way of getting their own back, giving me all that wind. Why on earth had I done such a crazy thing – even if it was in my sleep? It wasn't as if I was a sleepwalker. Gareth did that a lot, and talked complete rubbish in his sleep as well, which could be quite funny. But sleepwalking isn't funny. It can be downright dangerous. Gareth fell downstairs once and smashed his nose in. There was blood all over the place. And I'd gone downstairs head first – as a sheep! I was lucky to be alive.

By lunchtime, I was starving, but I really didn't fancy the burger and chips I usually have.

"Same as usual, Dewi?" asked Mrs Huws, the dinner lady, aiming her tongs at the greasy burgers.

"Um, no, not today Mrs Huws," I said.

"Oh. What do you fancy then, love?"

"Um … vegetable quiche and salad please." She gave me a funny look, then passed me a plate of limp lettuce with a few thin slices of tomatoes, so thin I could see the plate through them. She dumped a slice of quiche on top.

The lads gave me equally funny looks when I sat down with them. They had all piled their plates with the usual burgers, chips and sea of ketchup.

"Lettuce?!" said Jonno. "What's up? You on a diet or something?"

"I just didn't fancy a burger today."

"Yeah, but rabbit food? And quiche?" laughed Gwynfor. "That's girly food!"

"They had lamb stew today," said Bryn Hafod slowly (he always does everything slowly). "Why didn't you have that?"

Lamb stew? I felt sick.

"Um … no, I just felt like salad today, that's all. Anybody see the match last night?"

Football is always a good way of changing the subject. After dissecting the game for five minutes, the conversation went all over the place: from why Jonno's feet stink so bad, to the report on the radio that morning that some people had seen the mysterious big black cat again, only twenty miles away this time.

"But they were only some tourists from London, so you can hardly take them seriously," said Gwynfor.

"Why shouldn't we take Londoners seriously?" asked Jonno.

"Because they're not used to living in the country are they, you drong. Can't tell the difference between a rabbit and a sheep, can they?"

"But there are loads of cats in London, aren't there?" said Bryn (slowly).

"Exactly," said Jonno, "and I'm sure they'd know the difference between a small, ordinary domestic cat and a big, massive, dangerous one."

"Are you trying to tell me that you believe these stories about a black panther roaming around Wales?" asked Gwynfor.

"No, but there's never fire without smoke is there?"

"You mean smoke without fire, you div," I said.

"That's what I said! Anyway, there's always a reason for everything, so there must be a reason why you've started eating rabbit food all of a sudden ... What's wrong, Dews? Getting a bit podgy are we? Thought I spotted a good spare tyre there..."

"Oh, shut it."

Sometimes, even football doesn't change the subject around enough. And I most definitely do not have a spare tyre. I don't have an ounce of fat on me and I'm working really hard on my six-pack. OK, it's not quite there yet, but it's bigger than a three-pack, and it's definitely more than Jonno's! And by drawing attention to that, I managed to get them off talking about lettuce. Well, that's what I hoped, anyway.

CHAPTER 2

AFTER SCHOOL, I WENT straight to play with the dogs as usual, but they started barking furiously at me. Every single one of them – even Floss, who thinks the world of me. She usually lies on her back when she sees me walking towards her, whimpers until I tickle her belly, then she jumps up and licks my face. But now, she was looking at me as if she wanted to eat me. So I headed for the house, and I could have sworn the sheep were giving me funny looks as I passed.

Dad was in the kitchen having his tea: five jam sandwiches, two scones and a massive piece of sponge cake.

"Right then, Dewi and Gareth, go and get changed," he said. "I want you to help me dose the lambs."

So we changed into our work clothes and followed him to the yard where the lambs were waiting for us in the pens. They started bleating when they saw Dad and Gareth, but went all quiet when I arrived. Gareth and Dad didn't notice, but I did, and I started sweating again.

I was given the job of catching the lambs so that Dad could stuff the dosing gun into their mouths. I could feel them trembling with fear in my arms and I started feeling a bit emotional. There were tears in my eyes, but I tried telling myself that it was the wind blowing dust into my eyes, or that I'd suddenly become sensitive to the chemicals in the dosing solution. Dad didn't blink an eyelid anyway.

By the sixth lamb, I decided to whisper into his ear (the lamb, not Dad), and would you believe it? It worked. The lamb stopped trembling and from then on, every lamb came obediently towards me instead of struggling and bleating as they usually do. Dad noticed this after a while, but he didn't really say anything, only gave me a funny look and mumbled something about Dr Doolittle. Yeah, very funny …

We finished the dosing so quickly, Dad was in a really good mood. I was pretty chuffed too, until he asked me to go and feed the dogs. That's usually my favourite job, but this time I came out in goose bumps. I couldn't get out of it without drawing attention to myself though, and I didn't want to do that, did I?

I went into the shed to fetch a bucketful of the cornflake stuff and mixed it with hot water until it looked like multicoloured porridge.

Then I went out to face the dogs. They usually wag their tails and whimper and smile when they see me coming with the bucket and a trail of steam behind me, but this time, they were all growling.

I have never been afraid of dogs – until now. I'd never really noticed their teeth before – they're more like fangs – sharp, yellow, crocodilish and horrible. I was shaking. I swallowed hard and walked on towards Floss. She went nuts – and jumped towards me, her teeth like castanets. I jumped back. This wasn't going to be easy.

In the end, I had to fetch the yard brush so that I could use it to drag the food bowls towards me, fill them at a safe distance and then push them back within the dogs' reach. Unfortunately, Gareth passed just as I was shoving the very last bowl towards Nel.

"What are you doing, you nutter?!" he asked. "Are you scared of Nel or something?"

"Um … Just playing."

He stared at me for a long, long time, then shook his head and headed for the house, muttering something about "losing it … fruit cake …"

We had lasagne for supper – lamb lasagne. I tried to put a forkful in my mouth, but couldn't stop myself from gagging. Mam must have noticed.

"What's wrong?"

"Nothing. I'm just not hungry."

"You're always hungry! What's wrong with my lasagne? You love it, usually!"

"I know, and honest, there's nothing wrong with it, I just … well … I don't feel like it."

"Don't be silly, eat it, or do I have to remind you of all the little children starving in Africa?"

Mam hadn't mentioned that for years, not since we were small, when we refused to eat cabbage and broccoli. I blushed.

"Mam, look, I would love to eat it (liar, liar, pants on fire) but I can't, not tonight."

"Why not? Are you ill or something?"

"Could be. My stomach's a bit funny."

That was a mistake. Mam went straight to the medicine cabinet and came back with the bottle of Kaolin and Morphine that had been fermenting there for years, and made me swallow two spoonfuls of the disgusting stuff. It tasted like chalk.

'There's a good film on tonight," said Gareth, "*An American Werewolf in Paris*."

I'd never seen it before, and it was quite funny – until the bit where the bloke starts turning into a werewolf. Gareth was killing himself laughing, but I didn't think it was funny – not at all. I started psyching again. What was going to happen to me in bed that night? Would I turn into a sheep again, or was it just a 24-hour blip in my life? I convinced myself that I had nothing to worry about, and went to bed early – before the end of the film – so that I could fall asleep fairly quickly and forget about the worst day of my life so far and the fact that I was starving. I didn't really want to know what eventually happened to the man who turned into a werewolf either.

Of course, I didn't fall asleep for ages. I was scared, really scared, and kept looking at my arms, just to check that they weren't suddenly sprouting wool again. My empty stomach was making strange noises as well. But in the end, because I was exhausted, I suppose, I fell asleep. I woke up when Gareth tripped over my trainers on the way to bed, but I fell asleep again straight away, no problem. I really thought I was going to be OK.

But at about two in the morning, I started to feel hot and sweaty again. I'd peeled off my pyjamas before I'd even woken up properly. I nearly yelled out loud when I felt a sharp, shooting pain in my back and stomach, but

I didn't want to wake Gareth, so I ran to the bathroom and closed the door behind me. I fell to the floor, writhing in pain. That's when I noticed my hands … They weren't hands any more and my legs and arms were itching like mad – which wasn't surprising – curly white fluff was sprouting up all over them, and my legs were shrinking before my eyes and turning into horrible little stumps. It was happening again.

I jumped up so that my front legs were in the sink and I could see myself in the mirror. Yes, it was a sheep's face with a sheep nose, sheep ears and a mouthful of sheep teeth. 'Noooooo!' I groaned, but what came out was a long, doleful 'Baaaaaah!' I started crying, but that only came out as more bleating which made me want to cry even more.

It was strange. There was enough of me in me to have the sense to shut up before I woke the whole house, but I was dying to eat, to stuff myself silly. I knew it wasn't a good idea, but a force much stronger than myself was dragging me downstairs. At least Mam hadn't bought any new plants yet. I went all round the house and realised there was nothing I could eat there. But I knew where there would be proper grub.

I went out through the back door (I was

struggling with the handle until I realised I could grab it with my teeth and pull down hard) and into the garden. Mam's garden, with a big square patch of lovely, luscious lawn. I started grazing happily. I knew this wouldn't bother Mam and it definitely wouldn't bother Dad; he wouldn't have to mow it now. I had given the whole patch a No. 1 cut in no time at all, but I was still hungry.

That's when I noticed the lupins and lilies and alliums. I knew I shouldn't, but they seemed to be calling me, honest. I had no choice, and oh boy, were they tasty, especially the alliums. Just like cheese and onion crisps. Before long, there wasn't a single petal left, and I was still hungry.

I realised I was being watched – by a whole field of sheep. Their eyes were red glows in the darkness beyond the fence. I nearly jumped out of my skin – well, my wool. But then I realised that there was a big field of grass waiting for me on the other side of the fence. Unfortunately, because my Mam is obsessed with her garden, the fence was in pretty good nick and much too high for me to jump over. Rats. But then I remembered that the wooden gate by the main road was a bit rotten. Hah! So I trotted off along the lane and down the main road. One good kick with my back legs and there was a hole big enough for me to squeeze through. I grazed and grazed and then had a very contented lie down. That's when I realised that the other sheep had gathered around me in a large semi circle.

"Hi," I said in my best bleat. But nobody answered. They just stood there, staring at me. "What's up? Never seen a sheep grazing before?"

"You're not a sheep," said one huffily.

"No, I agree, this is only temporary. Well, I hope it's temporary."

"What are you on about?" sniffed the huffy one, "You're not a sheep – you're a ram."

A ram?! I hadn't thought of that, but of course I was a ram: I'm a boy, aren't I?

"You shouldn't be here with us," said the ewe, "not yet anyway. You naughty boy..." she added with a smile, and started coming closer with a Beyoncé-like wiggle of her backside. Oh dear. Oh dear oh dear oh dear. I could feel myself blushing under my wool, and was grateful that wool doesn't turn pink when a sheep – sorry – ram gets embarrassed. They couldn't tell how red I really was. But it soon got a whole lot worse.

"Oh, bless! He's not old enough!" laughed

an older ewe, "Look! He hasn't even grown any horns yet!"

The whole flock started laughing. I didn't know what to say so I turned my back on them and pretended to go to sleep. Unfortunately, my acting was too good, because I suddenly woke up and it was daytime and I was myself again – a normal boy, except that this normal boy was lying in a field, stark naked. AAAAAAAH!!

To the accompaniment of the bleating flock, I ran across the field towards the house, leapt over the fence, shot through the kitchen, remembering to slow down before climbing the stairs, turned on the landing and ran straight into ... Lowri. She gave me a funny look.

"Where's your pyjamas?" she asked.

"Um ..." I tried to hide what she was staring at.

"And what were you doing in the field? I saw you. You were lying there with no clothes on."

"It wasn't me!"

"Yes it was, look at your feet – and your hands, you're all dirty!"

She was right. I couldn't deny it, and there were dirty footprints all the way up the stairs. Mam would go mental again.

"I must have been walking in my sleep."

"But Gareth is the only one who …"

"Yes, well, I must have caught the bug or something. Lowri, you won't tell anybody, will you?"

"We'll see …"

The little cow! She was giving me one of those sly looks of hers!

"Oh come on Lowri, please!"

"Like I said, we'll see. You'll have to be really nice to me won't you?" The cheeky little minx was trying to blackmail me!

"What do you mean, be nice to you?"

"I'll think of something. Now go and put some clothes on. You'll catch cold …"

And off she went to the bathroom. I wanted to break the door down, I was so angry. But I didn't. I opened the bedroom door instead – very carefully, and tried to get into bed without waking Gareth. I was under the sheets before I remembered I was all muddy and dirty. Oh no … Mam was going to skin me alive.

At least it was Saturday, and I wouldn't have to go to school. But my stomach hurt – more farts, yet again, desperate to get out.

CHAPTER 3

DAD TOLD ME OFF for getting up so late. He's always really chirpy in the mornings and expects everybody else to be the same. I'm usually quite good, much better than Gareth, but I hadn't had much sleep, had I?

I sat at the table and reached for the box of cornflakes.

"You don't deserve breakfast after getting up so late!" said Dad.

"Don't be silly, John," said Mam, "the boy's still growing and needs a good breakfast. Leave him alone and open that door for me will you?" She was carrying a basket of washing to hang out on the line. Dad opened the door for her and gave me a dirty look.

"I'll help you, Mam," said Lowri in a silly little 'Aren't-I-a-good-little-girl-offering-to-help-her-mother-just-to-draw-attention-to-the-fact-that-her-brother-Dewi's-really-bad-for-getting-up-so-late?' voice. Cow.

Then a scream came from the garden.

It was like World War Three afterwards. Dad

and Gareth went out to see what the fuss was all about, and I stayed where I was. I had just remembered what I'd been doing in the garden. I could hear everything anyway. Mam was screaming blue murder and accusing everybody and everything of leaving gates open and being too stupid to put up decent fences and "Look at my lupins!" Dad was protesting and saying that he just couldn't understand it, until he saw that the gate to the field was wide open (O, oh…) and then he started accusing Gareth of not closing it. Gareth was yelling "Why do I always get the blame?!" and Lowri was crying because Mam was crying and I just wanted to crawl under the table and hide.

Then I heard Lowri's voice saying: "Dewi was in that field this morning … I saw him."

Silence. Then: "Dewi! Come out here this minute!"

I had no choice. I went out into the garden. Well, what was left of it. There were no flower heads left anywhere. There were hardly any leaves either.

"Well?" asked Dad, staring at me with those cold blue eyes of his, eyes that turn colder than blue Antarctic icebergs when he's angry. "Did you leave that gate open? Are you responsible for letting sheep into your mother's garden?"

"Um … yes and no." That was a mistake. Even his face was turning blue now.

"What do you mean, yes and no?! Give a straight answer to a straight question!"

"There were two questions there, Dad …"

"Answer both before I skin you alive!"

"Um … well … yes, I left the gate open, and I'm really sorry, Mam, but, um …" My throat went dry. I could never tell them what really happened. They would never believe me.

"UM, WHAT?!" exploded Dad.

"Um, yes, it was my fault. I left the gate open and it was me that let the sheep into the garden."

Dad has never hit any of us. One cold blue stare, and that's usually enough for us. We whither in front of him. Cry, sometimes. And he knows that we've learnt our lesson. But this time, he clipped me across the head. It hurt. We both stared at each other in shock. I think he was even more shocked than me.

Then Mam shouted at him: "John! There was no need to hit him! You big bully! Dewi? Are you alright?"

I sort of nodded and stared at my feet. Dad mumbled something and then walked off towards the yard.

We were all really quiet for the rest of the

day, and Dad wasn't speaking to me – nor my Mam. I went to town with her in the afternoon, to the garden centre. There wasn't a lot there, but Mam managed to spend £50 on some pretty feeble looking specimens.

"And of course, that will come out of your pocket money, Dewi." £50?! That meant I'd be skint for months! I had less pocket money than any of my mates as it was, and if that wasn't enough, she made me plant the whole lot when we came home. I hate planting flipping flowers. This sheep thing was becoming a real pain.

CHAPTER 4

ABOUT A WEEK LATER, I went for a walk after supper and climbed up my favourite tree so that I could have some peace and quiet. It's an enormous oak tree with wide branches, and when I was about ten, I tried to make myself a tree house in it. All I managed to do was nail two planks from one flattish branch to another, and rip the backside of my trousers on one of the nails a week later. Mam told me off so I sulked and didn't bother with any more DIY. But it still makes a good place to sit and ponder, well away from everybody else. And I really needed to be able to think just now.

Why had I suddenly started turning into a sheep? How was I ever going to stop turning into a stupid, idiotic, ravenous sheep? I had noticed that it was happening earlier every night and that I was staying in sheep form until later in the mornings too. Did this mean I'd be a sheep all day, every day, before long? I had to sort this out pretty quick. But how? I didn't have a clue. Maybe I should talk to somebody – but who?

"Dewi? What are you doing up there?"

Oh no. Lowri, staring at me from the foot of the tree. My tree.

"Go away."

"No, I won't go away. Help me up."

"Why should I?"

"Because I want to apologise."

"You just did. Now go away."

"Don't be like that. I'm sorry for dobbing you in about the gate."

"Too flipping right."

"But it was you, wasn't it?" I didn't bother answering. "Oh, come on. Help me up Dewi, please. I know something's wrong; you can tell me."

"You? You're only nine years old and you're a girl. How the heck could you help?"

"Aha. So something is definitely wrong. Help me up or I'll break my leg and you'll get the blame."

Little cow. But she was right. I reached down and dragged her up.

"You're getting heavy for a nine-year-old."

"Huh. It's you that's weak for a thirteen-year-old."

She sat beside me carefully.

"So what's wrong, Dewi? Why were you lying in a field with no clothes on?"

I took my time. Was I going to tell her? Or would she just laugh in my face? What would you have done if you were me?

"You're not going to believe me," I said at last.

"Come on, just spit it out."

"If you promise not to laugh; because it's not funny."

"Cross my heart and hope to die," she said, licking her middle finger and drawing it across her throat.

"And promise not to tell anyone else?"

"Promise."

"Nobody, not one single person in the whole world?"

"I swear on Mam's life!"

"OK. Right ... This is going to sound really stupid. I can hardly believe it myself, but it's true."

"Yes?"

"I've started turning into a sheep."

She stared at me for a while, then shook her head slowly and giggled.

"You promised not to laugh!"

"Yes, but you don't expect me to believe that! Come on, what's really the matter, Dewi?"

"I just told you! I turn into a sheep – every night – have done for days! And it's not flippin' funny!"

"But how can that happen?"

"I don't know! It just does!"

"You're probably dreaming."

"I am not! It really happens. Who do you think ate Mam's plants?"

"You never! Why?"

"BECAUSE I WAS A SHEEP!"

I was becoming a bit stroppy now.

"Look Dewi, just because I'm only nine years old, you don't have to treat me like an imbecile."

"I'm not! I'm telling you the truth!"

"No you're not. And I can't believe you'd expect me to be stupid enough to believe a silly story like that. Turning into a sheep ...!"

"I told you you wouldn't believe me, didn't I!"

"If you're going to keep shouting at me like that, I'm off. Help me down, please."

"You can go stuff yourself," I said, folding my arms.

"Alright then, I'll jump down, and if I break my leg it'll be all your fault."

"Hope you land on your head!"

"Oh, you're horrible ... I only wanted to help."

"And all you did was laugh and refuse to believe me!"

"If you can prove you're telling the truth, I might listen to you. But you can't, can you?"

She looked at me with that sucked up little mouth thing she does when she's making a point. So I made her wait ages before giving her an answer.

"You wait 'til tonight," I said eventually. "I'll come to your bedroom and then you'll see."

"Yeah, whatever …"

"And when you see that I'm telling the truth, take me out to the field to graze for a bit …"

"Graze?!"

"Yes, that's what sheep do … then bring me back in and make sure you close the gate behind us."

She stared at me for a while, saying nothing, then:

"Yes, of course I'll take you out for a … graze!" she said, rolling her eyeballs, "Now, are you going to help me down?"

"Promise?"

She rolled her eyes again, nodded, and I slowly lowered her down from the tree. But when she disappeared round the corner, I wanted to kick myself. I should have let her break her leg.

CHAPTER 5.

"Aaaaah!"

Typical. I should have known Lowri would react like that. But since I was a sheep, I couldn't tell her to shut her face, could I? She was staring at me from her pink bed, in her pink pyjamas, her hand still on the light switch of her pink table lamp. All that pink was making me feel sick, but I was determined to prove to her that I had been telling the truth.

"Dewi?" she whispered eventually, "Is that you?"

At last. I nodded.

"Prove it then. Prove that you're not just some bad sheep who happened to wander into my bedroom."

Oh boy. What sheep in its right mind would want to wander into her bedroom? And how on earth was I going to prove that it really was me? I bleated under my breath.

"Bleating isn't enough. Do something."

What did she expect me to do? Stand on my head and sing 'Land of My Fathers'? I was a sheep! I stamped my hooves in exasperation on the (pink) carpet and stepped towards her. She looked at me warily.

"That doesn't prove a thing. Do something Dewi would do."

So I gave her a head-butt.

"Ooooow!" She rubbed her forehead and then slapped me across my snout. "Dewi, you're such a meanie! There was no call for that, was there?"

Oh yes there was. She'd realised it was me now, hadn't she?

She put on her dressing gown and trainers (yes, all pink ...) and giggled.

"I don't believe this! You really were telling the truth! Oh my God! My brother's a sheep! That is so funny ..."

She'd get another head-butt in a minute.

Eventually, we were out of the house and wandering around the field: I was starving. I'd had to eat some of the beef burger we had for supper, but I'd managed to slip most of it into my pocket without anybody noticing and had thrown it (from a distance) to the dogs later on. I didn't dare put it in the bin in case Mam found it.

I don't know if other Mams examine the contents of bins, but my Mam has X-ray eyes. I broke one of her ornaments once, and was too much of a coward to own up, so I wrapped all the bits in a newspaper and stuffed it right to the bottom of the bin. Yes, she found it, and I still don't know how.

Anyway, I stuffed myself with lovely, lush grass for ages. Because Lowri was with me, the other sheep kept their distance, but I could hear them bleating snide comments from the other end of the field. Sheep can be really nasty – and cheeky. If I repeated some of the things they were saying, you'd blush. But Lowri was prattling on in my other ear.

"How long are you going to be a sheep then? I'm bored now. O heck, yeah, you can't answer me, can you? Couldn't you nod or something? Did you just shake your head then? Why? You can't be bothered, can you? Does that grass taste nice? A bit like spinach or cabbage I suppose. I still can't believe I have a brother who's a sheep … a real live sheep. And you've got such nice, clean wool. Let me just have a touch …" She started stroking my shoulders then, scratching my head and stuff. If felt quite nice, actually.

"Oh, you're really fluffy. If you stay a sheep until summer, do you think they'll shear you?"

I nearly choked. I hadn't thought of that. Shear me?! My head wedged between my dad's legs, or even worse, Ifan Jones, who's a speed shearer and a real butcher? He'd cut me to ribbons! Obviously, they don't shear in the middle of the night, but I was definitely turning into sheep form earlier every night, an hour earlier this time, and if this was going to be a regular pattern, I'd soon be a sheep all day too. I started trembling.

"You're so much nicer as a sheep, you know," said Lowri. "I can talk to you properly and you don't answer back and say nasty things to me."

Talk to me properly? She was doing my head in, not just scratching it!

"Ooh!" she said suddenly. "What are these hard bits on either side of your head? Hey – you're growing horns, Dewi! You're turning into a ram!"

Oh no ...

CHAPTER 6

By the time I turned back into human form that morning, it was almost seven, and Lowri had fallen asleep by my side in the field. Rats, she was supposed to have taken me back in after a quick graze – and now I was naked in a field again! I managed to take off her dressing gown before waking her. Well, I needed to hide my crown jewels somehow, didn't I?

"Uh? Where am I?" she asked sleepily as I helped her to her feet.

"In the field. And now we're going back into the house, so keep quiet, we don't want to wake anyone."

"Oh yes, I remember now. You turned into a sheep."

"Yes, and you promised not to tell. We'll talk about it later. Now come on."

I managed to get into bed without waking Gareth, but just couldn't get back to sleep. I was worrying too much. I kept seeing images of myself being shorn over and over again, being thrown head first into the sheep dip, being squashed into an Ifor Williams trailer with loads of other sheep and being sold in the mart to Jones the butcher … I had to stop this sheep stuff before it was too late!

"Why are you grunting like that?" asked Gareth, and he didn't sound happy. "You ill or something?"

"No."

"Shut up then."

So I did. And then Mam started using her saucepans as a drum kit downstairs.

"Gareth-Dewi-Lowri! Breakfast!"

Because it was Sunday, she had fried a mountain of bacon and eggs for us, and Dad was already stuffing his face when we came down. The smell was almost too much for me.

"Just cornflakes for me, please, Mam."

"Again?" she asked in surprise. "Are you ill?"

"No," I said, giving Lowri a sharp look because she was smiling inanely.

"But something's definitely wrong," said Mam, putting her hand on my forehead. "You haven't been yourself for days."

Lowri started giggling so I gave her a sharp kick under the table.

"All I know is, there's a funnier smell than usual in the bedroom every morning," said

38

Gareth, with an accusing look at me. "And it's nothing to do with me."

"What kind of smell?" asked Dad, his mouth full of egg sandwich.

"Dunno. Just different."

"I'm not surprised," said Mam. "I haven't been able to clean the place for weeks, because I can't see the carpet! It's time you two sorted out your rubbish so that I can hoover in there."

"Something for you to do after breakfast then, lads?" said Dad.

"Uh? But it's Sunday," said Gareth, "supposed to be a day of rest."

"If you've turned religious all of a sudden, you can go to chapel this afternoon too," said Dad.

That made Gareth shut up pretty quick.

So, even though it was a beautiful day outside, Gareth and I had to stay inside, clearing up the bedroom. I hate tidying, and was trying my best to get it over with, but Mam kept poking her head in.

"Don't you dare try stuffing everything under the bed, Dewi! I want to be able to hoover under there too! And here you go – polish and duster – I want to see those cupboards gleaming. And bring me your bedclothes – they'll dry in no time on the line today."

I tried folding my sheets so that she couldn't see the dirt all over them, but, like I said, that woman has X-ray eyes.

"Dewi! What on earth? Look at the state of these sheets!"

"Um ..."

"What have you been doing? Swimming in mud before going to bed? When did you last have a shower?"

"Um ..."

"Show me your feet! Come on! Take those trainers off this minute!"

"But, Mam ..."

"Now!" I had no choice, and of course, my feet were disgusting after grazing in the field all night.

"So that's where the smell comes from ..." smiled Gareth, smug as a smug thing on smug tablets.

"Shower! Now!" screamed Mam. "And scrub between those toes! I can't believe this. You're thirteen now, Dewi, and you still haven't learnt to wash yourself properly! What's wrong with you, uh?"

"Dipstick," said Gareth.

"Oh, leave him alone," said Lowri from the landing, "he's just going through a difficult phase, that's all."

"What are you on about – 'difficult phase'?" sniffed Gareth.

"He's at that awkward age, isn't he? On the border between being a child and a young man in his teens, and ..."

"What would you know about stuff like that?" sniggered Gareth. "You're only nine and you're talking just like a middle-aged teacher!"

"I know these things because I read, Gareth. It would do you good to read a bit too, you know. You might learn something and be able to talk about interesting subjects, not just football for a change."

We all stared at her in silence for a bit. Then:

"You scare me sometimes, Lowri," said Mam.

"Me too," said Gareth, "and if reading makes somebody think and talk like you, I'd rather be a thicko."

"Moron," said Lowri, turning sharply and walking away with her nose in the air. She scared me too, but at least she'd managed to make Mam forget about my filthy bed sheets.

I managed to have a word with her after lunch, when she came to the foot of the oak tree again.

"Well? Managed to get your incredible IQ in

gear?" I asked after dragging her up to join me. "Any idea why I've started turning into a sheep and how to stop it happening?"

"Well ..." she said slowly and ever-so-importantly, "I've been thinking about it all night as it happens."

"And?"

"You should go and see the doctor."

"What?! Don't be daft! No doctor is going to believe me, are they? Even if they did, I don't want to be like ET in the film, all tubes and stuff. I'm not going to see a doctor until ... until it's deadly serious."

"If you wait until it's deadly serious, you'll need a vet, not a doctor."

"Ha ha. Very funny. Not. But why do you think this is happening to me? Why not you or Gareth?"

"Well ... you did fall into the sheep dip last year, didn't you? Maybe your body's reacting to the chemicals or something."

"But most farmers get a bit of sheep dip over them at some point, and they don't turn into sheep!"

"As far as we know ..."

"Don't be silly!"

"OK, calm down; I'm just thinking it through. Now, d'you remember Mam saying you used to

42

eat sheep droppings when you were little?"

"Lots of kids do that!"

"I never did. What made you do it anyway?"

"How should I know? I was only little. I probably thought they were currants or something."

"Didn't you use to swig the pet lamb's bottle as well? One swig for you and one for the lamb, Dad said."

"What? You think the germs did something to me?"

"I don't know, do I? Maybe it's a combination of all those things. Maybe it was too much for you."

"Sorry, Lowri, but no way. There must be some other explanation. And how come you know words like 'combination' anyway? You're only nine! It's not normal."

"Oh, listen to the bloke who turns into a sheep every night ..."

She started rubbing her chin like some clever professor, to show that she was thinking really hard now. "OK," she said finally, "if you don't believe any of those reasons, let's think of something else. When people turn into vampires or werewolves, they've usually been bitten. Have you ever been bitten by a sheep?"

"Lowri ... don't be silly – sheep don't bite!"

"But they've got teeth."

That's when I remembered that a stroppy ewe lamb had given me a nip a couple of months earlier. It didn't hurt, but the teeth marks were there for a while. Lowri folded her arms with a smirk.

"There you go! That's obviously what happened!"

"Maybe, but we don't know for definite, do we? And even if that is the answer, how do I stop it from happening again?"

"Well, if we keep going with the vampire and werewolf thing, you need to be shot with a silver bullet or have a stake rammed into you."

"Yeah, but that tended to kill them, didn't it?"

"Yes."

"But I don't want to die!"

"Do you want to be half boy, half sheep for the rest of your life?"

"'Course not! But I definitely don't want you stabbing me with a stake either! And anyhow, vampires and werewolves are – were – whatever – dangerous things that eat people. I'm an innocent lamb who's done no harm at all to anyone!"

"I'm not sure Mam's plants would agree with

you. And you've really upset her, haven't you? Come to think of it, maybe we should tell Mam and Dad, they might know what to do."

"No way am I telling them!"

In the end, we decided that the best plan of action was to go on the Internet in the town library, and see if anything like this had ever happened to anyone else, anywhere on the planet.

CHAPTER 7

A WEEK LATER, WE still didn't have a clue. I'd found facts about people who'd been born with hair all over them, and people who started looking like their pets, but there was nothing at all about people who had suddenly started turning into sheep.

"Don't worry, Dewi," said Lowri, "I'm bound to think of something in the end."

In the end? The end might be too late!

I was beginning to panic now. I was turning into a sheep even earlier every night and staying a sheep until later every morning. Gareth was going to wake up any day now, and find a sheep next to him. But the worst thing was: I had grown horns – which wouldn't go away. They were only stumpy little things, not big, curly ones – yet, but they were getting bigger and bigger and a good couple of centimetres already. Lucky my hair's really thick and spiky. But I'd started wearing a hat just in case, a red, woolly one with 'Wales' on it, but it was getting warmer now, so it was hot, sweaty and itchy.

I kept scratching my head all the time. It was obviously getting on Menna Morgan's nerves.

"Why don't you take that silly hat off?" she asked sniffily in French class.

"Because I don't want to."

"But you haven't stopped scratching since you sat down."

"I can scratch if I want to. There's no law against it!"

"But it's getting on my nerves. Have you got fleas or something?"

"Don't be stupid."

"Dewi and Menna!" shrieked Mlle Jones, nearly giving us heart attacks. "How many times do I have to repeat myself? *Taisez-vous! C'est moi qui parle!*" I didn't understand the French but I got the gist of the tone of voice. She wanted us to shut up. So we did, and concentrated on talking about the weather in French. '*Il fait chaud*', yes, 'It's hot' and I was *très, très chaud*. I was melting.

Ten minutes later, Menna had had enough.

"Will you stop that horrible scratching! I can't concentrate!" she whispered.

"Tough!" I whispered back.

"What's wrong? Not washed your hair today?"

"What do you mean, today? I only wash it

once a week."

"Oh, yuk! That's disgusting!"

"Come off it. You never wash yours every day, do you?"

"Of course I do. Doesn't everybody?"

"No, Menna, they don't. You've obviously got some kind of hygiene obsession."

"Well if I have, it's not surprising, having to sit next to you three times a week!"

"Dewi and Menna!" screamed Mlle Jones, "*Répétez ce que je viens de dire!*"

"Pardon?"

"Repeat – *répétez* – what I just said!"

"Um …"

"*Bon*, come and see me at the end of the lesson."

We both had detention for the whole of the lunch break. Brilliant. A whole hour with just Menna Morgan and Mlle Jones. Everybody else was outside playing cricket.

"This is all your fault," hissed Menna, brushing her hair for the twentieth time.

"No way, you're the one who started fussing."

"Only because you were scratching like some mangy dog next to me! And you stink too!"

"I stink? I had a bath last night, thank you!"

I'd been grazing out in the field all night after

48

the bath, but I wasn't going to tell her that, was I?"

"Well you're obviously not using enough soap or you're sleeping with a whole flock of sheep, because you smell just like one!"

"Uh? Sheep don't smell!" She looked at me with pity and shook her head.

"That just goes to show what a right flipping farmer you are."

"Oi! What's so 'flipping' about being a farmer? I'm glad I live on a farm!"

"Good. I'm glad I don't!"

She must have really felt it, because she threw her arm out wildly just as she said that, and managed to send a big pile of books flying over the floor. I leant over quickly to try and save them, but so did she. So we met in the middle – forehead to forehead – with a massive crack. I saw stars for a while. She probably did, too.

"Sorry, are you OK?" I asked, rubbing my sore forehead.

"No, I'm not. You have a head like a brick wall."

"Yours isn't exactly made of sponge, either."

"No. Course not. Sorry." And she smiled at me.

Our heads were still quite close together, and for the very first time, I noticed her eyes. They were a really weird colour.

"Hey, your eyes are cool," I said without thinking.

"Yeah?"

"Yes, they're yellow."

"Don't be a dork. They're green with a bit of brown: hazel."

"No way. Those are yellow. Totally yellow."

"No they're not!"

"I'm telling you they are! I'm the one who can see them, not you!"

"Well you obviously need glasses then," she said stroppily, "They're hazel, OK? The light must be funny in here or something. Come to think of it, your eyes look different too."

"They do?"

"They're a really dark brown."

"So? They've always been brown."

"Not as brown as that."

"Oh." I wanted to say more, but the bell went.

We had games after lunch: athletics. I'm quite good at sprinting, always get picked for the relay team, at least, and I can chuck the javelin a fair way, but I'm no Colin Jackson. Rugby's more my game, to be honest. But this time, I – and Mr Ap Iwan, the games teacher – had the shock of our lives. We were all having a go at every event, and the first one was the long jump. When I jumped, it was as if somebody had put springs inside my legs. I flew through the air for ages before landing on all fours in the sand pit. The lads were all dumbstruck, and Ap Iwan went bonkers.

"Don't move!" he said, "We have to measure that one!" He took a tape measure out of his pocket and went to work. Over five metres. "What's happened to you, Dewi?" he asked, with a gleam in his eyes.

"Um … Don't know, Sir."

But I had a good idea. I pulled my hat lower over my ears and followed him to the high jump. The same thing happened there; I sailed over the bar at 1.80m, with loads to spare. Ap Iwan was getting really excited by now.

"Amazing! Astounding! I don't get it! You weren't this good last year, Dewi. Have you been practising in secret or something?"

"No, Sir."

"Are you sure?"

"Honest, Sir."

"Dewi … you haven't been … taking steroids have you?"

"What? No, Sir!"

"Hm. Well, in that case, if you carry on like this, I can see you getting to the Welsh

Championships this year. How's your sprinting, I wonder? Lads! The 100 metres! Come on!"

I beat the others by miles, even Jonno, who's like a whippet. The same thing happened with the 200 and 400 metres. I thought it might be wiser for me to slow down, I didn't want to draw too much attention to myself, after all, but I just couldn't stop myself from running. It was such a brilliant feeling, running like the wind, flying past all the others, and seeing their faces afterwards, especially Jonno's. I couldn't stop grinning.

"What the heck's happened to you?" asked Bryn. "You never used to be able to run like that."

"No, there's something fishy about it," said Jonno. "And your running style's really weird too. How can you run so fast when you're leaning forward like that, almost on all fours?"

"We all have our different styles," I said with a smile. OK, a smug smile.

That's when I noticed that the girls were getting ready to start sprinting too. Menna Morgan was in the start position, ready for the 'On your marks, get set …'

"Go!" yelled Miss Humphreys, and off they went. Wow. The other girls were running like … well, girls, arms flailing like windmills and feet pointing in all directions, and some with their boobs bouncing around. But Menna Morgan was running as if her feet weren't touching the ground, running as smooth and perfect as velvet. She had real style. She passed the finishing line before the others even got half way.

"Could she run like that last year?" I asked the boys.

"Menna Morgan? Oh yes, definitely," said Gwynfor. "She broke the junior 100 metres record – and the 200 as well. I remember thinking it was strange because she was like a fart in primary school. Funny how people change when they get to secondary. The muscles must develop overnight or something. Maybe that's what's happened to you, Dewi."

"Yeah, something like that, I suppose," I said, watching Menna fly round the corner, well ahead in the 200 too.

CHAPTER 8

I DON'T KNOW IF all that running and jumping had something to do with it, but I started turning into a sheep much earlier that night. I could feel the strange heat and itching coming over me straight after supper.

"Um, I think I'll go for a bath," I said loudly, glancing at Lowri.

"Good idea," said Gareth. "You stink." Sometimes, there's just no point reacting, is there? So I didn't.

I rushed upstairs and shut the bedroom door tightly behind me. There was no point having a bath, I was about to turn into a sheep – my feet were already becoming smaller and harder and my head was starting to change shape. What was I going to do? Gareth would come in at some point and switch on the light (he's not the most considerate of room mates). I could try hiding completely under the bedclothes, but he'd still be able to see I was a funny shape. I was beginning to panic now and sweating like a pig (well, a sheep), when somebody knocked lightly on the door. Oh no!

"Dewi? It's me," said Lowri through the keyhole, "Let me in."

"No chance!" I didn't want to turn into a sheep right in front of her. It's not a pretty sight, and she's only nine years old, after all. It might affect her for the rest of her life.

"Oh come on, I know what's happening!"

"But I'm half way through it – and it's not nice."

"Huh. I've seen you naked, remember." Charming. The girl was getting too cheeky for her own good. "Dewi! Let me in – before you change completely, or we won't be able to talk, will we?"

She was right – as usual. I opened the door.

"Oh my God!" she whimpered, clapping her hand over her mouth. "You're half and half!" My feet and arms had transformed completely, my nose had grown and wool was sprouting all over the rest of me. "Oh yuk, that's so disgusting!"

"Thanks, Lowri. Just what I wanted to hear. Right, what am I going to do? Gareth is going to see me."

"Want to sleep in my room? You can squeeze under my bed until Mam goes to bed."

"But Gareth will notice I'm not in my own

bed, won't he?"

"We can stuff loads of clothes under the sheets so it looks like you. Come on, hurry."

"You'll have to do it on your own. I don't have any hands."

"Oh, no you don't ... sorry."

Fair play, she did a pretty good job of making a human shape under the duvet, and by the time she'd finished, I was a sheep from head to toe. Not that sheep have toes, but you know what I mean. We went into her bedroom where I squeezed under her bed and stayed put – for ages. The carpet was covered in dust and fluff and I was dying to sneeze. Lowri prattled on above me non-stop, and if that wasn't enough, she started playing some horrible girly-band on her CD player. I screamed at her to switch it off, but what came out was a horrible, strangulated bleat.

"Dewi!" she hissed, "Shut up or Mam will hear you!"

Hear me over the bleating of those silly little girlies? I doubted that very much, but I shut my mouth and kicked the mattress instead

"Dewi ... behave," said the little Madam in her best teacher voice. "Now, I know you're not comfy down there and feeling thoroughly frustrated," (Thoroughly frustrated?! Did this nine-year-old eat dictionaries or something?) "and you're probably worried sick. I really think we should tell Mam and Dad."

What? I gave another, harder kick. Tell Mam and Dad?! No way! I didn't want them to know!

"Ouch! Give over, you! Now listen … at this rate, you'll be a sheep all day long in no time, and what if Dad sees you and takes you to the mart? He'd never believe me if I tried to tell him that you were that ram trembling in the corner, would he? Shouldn't think the butcher would believe me either …"

I swallowed – hard. I could be lamb chops, swimming in gravy and mint sauce. Or skewered on a barbecue. Or my leg could be Sunday lunch.

"That's shaken you up a bit, hasn't it?" she said in a kinder voice, "I can feel it. You're trembling, aren't you?"

I was like a slug on a washing machine on full spin cycle.

"So," she went on, "if you let me tell Mam and Dad, kick the mattress once, twice if you don't."

I didn't have to think. I kicked.

"Great. You're doing the right thing, Dewi, trust me. Right, when Mam comes in, I'll tell her, and you can come out from under the bed. I don't think we should try telling everybody at the same time, and come to think of it, I'm not sure we should tell Gareth at all. You know what he's like."

Oh yes. I knew only too well.

At about ten o'clock, Mam came in.

"You alright there, Lowri? Brushed your teeth?"

"Yes, Mam. Um …"

"Yes?"

"Uhh … there's something I want to tell you and I think you'd better sit down first."

"Oh?" Mam sat on the bed, right on top of me. I could feel the springs cutting into me.

"No! Not there! Over there, on the chair."

I saw Lowri's pink little feet scurrying across the room to take her clothes off the wooden chair by the window, and then Mam's sheepskin slippers following them. She sat down with a groan.

"What have you done, Lowri?"

"Me? Nothing!"

"So what's up?"

"Well … you know the funny things that have been happening recently? Your flowers and the plants and stuff?"

"Yes …" She sounded suspicious straight away.

"And you've noticed that Dewi's not been himself for a while now …"

"Yes …"

"Well, I'm afraid that something quite serious and rather unfortunate has happened to him."

"Something very serious and most unfortunate will happen to him if he had anything to do with my plants!"

"Mam! Listen, please … yes, he was sort of responsible, but it wasn't his fault, because … well … don't be scared, and please don't scream, but … Dewi? Come out."

Oh. My Life … I was trembling uncontrollably by now and sweating pints. I dragged myself out, lifted my head and tried to smile at Mam.

"What the —?" she shrieked and jumped to her feet.

"Mam! Shush. I asked you not to scream."

"But there's a sheep in your bedroom!"

"That isn't actually a sheep."

"Bit big for a cat, isn't it? Lowri! How long have you been keeping a sheep under your bed?!"

"Listen, it isn't a sheep. It's a ram. And it's not really a ram either. I know it looks like a ram – or sheep – whatever – but it's actually, I swear, your son. That's Dewi, Mam."

I don't think I had ever seen Mam looking quite so shocked before. She stared at Lowri, she stared at me, then back at Lowri, then collapsed onto the chair. She wasn't sure whether she should laugh or get really angry, I could tell by the way her mouth was making funny shapes.

"This isn't funny, Lowri."

"No, Mam, it's not, not funny at all. It's very serious and that's why we've decided to tell you, so that you can help us."

"Huh?"

"Mam, your son turns into a sheep every night and he's got horns growing out of his head."

"Lowri, listen," said Mam slowly, getting back on her feet carefully. "I'm really glad that you enjoy books so much and that you've got such a lively imagination, but this is getting out of hand now. This sheep is leaving your bedroom before it starts peeing all over the carpet ... come on, help me." And she walked towards me, grabbed a handful of fleece on the back of my neck and started dragging me towards the door.

"Dewi! Do something to prove it's you!" squeaked Lowri in a panic.

Good idea. But what? I looked at Mam and she looked at me. So I licked her leg. I would have licked her hand but I couldn't reach.

"Oh! Yuk! What have you been teaching this sheep?"

"Dewi! Go to the bookshelf and point your

60

nose at *Charlie and the Chocolate Factory*!" said Lowri quickly.

So I did, and then turned towards Mam and tried to smile again.

"That doesn't prove a thing. And why does it keeping baring its teeth like that? Does this sheep think it's a dog?"

"He's smiling, Mam! Dewi, open the wardrobe door and pull out my red coat."

Fine, another good idea. I grabbed the handle with my teeth and pulled. A red coat? There were so many clothes in there, I couldn't see any red coat. I rifled through the whole lot with my nose and finally found it. I sunk my teeth into it and yanked. The whole wardrobe nearly fell on top of me.

"Well? Do you believe me now?" asked Lowri.

"I'm not … I can't … Oh dear, I don't know what to … you could have trained this sheep to … but, no … Dewi?"

Poor old Mam. She'd gone all pale and had to sit down again. I walked towards her, licked her hand and placed my chin on her lap, looking into her eyes just like I used to when I was a little boy.

"It's you!" she whispered. "I recognise your eyes now. Oh, Dewi!" And she started crying.

"Please don't cry, Mam!" said Lowri, who looked as if she was on the verge of tears herself.

"But I don't … how … why has Dewi turned into a sheep?" asked Mam as she stroked my head gently.

"We don't know. It's been happening for a while now. He used to change in the middle of the night and be himself again before sunrise, but he's started changing earlier every night and we can't tell when he'll change back again tomorrow."

"This makes no sense! How can a boy turn into a sheep all of a sudden?"

Lowri went through all the possible reasons we'd talked about already: the fact that I'd fallen into the sheep dip last year, that I used to eat sheep droppings and drink from the pet lamb's bottle when I was a toddler.

"And you think the effect of all that's built up over the years? That's ridiculous!"

"Almost as ridiculous as having a sheep for a son!"

Lowri was getting just a tiny bit stroppy. But fair play to Mam, this was all a massive shock to her. Other mothers have to cope with their sons turning into yobs and hooligans or joy riders or something, not into sheep that scoff their favourite plants.

"There has to be some reasonable explanation," said Mam, "or ... are you two just pulling my leg? It's a fancy dress costume isn't it? You mean little devil, come here!" And she started yanking at my horns and tried to twist my head off! I yelled – which came out as a horrific bleat, of course.

"Mam!" hissed Lowri, "Stop it! You're hurting him! And look at him properly – does that look like a fancy dress costume?"

"I don't know ... they can make things look very realistic these days."

"But look at his mouth!" protested Lowri, prising my lips apart. "Look! Real sheep teeth, a real wet, sticky sheep tongue. Even Steven Spielberg couldn't do that!"

Mam looked and then half collapsed to the floor. She sat there like a rag doll, looking ten years older.

"I don't know what to think. It's so ..."

"I know. I had a shock too. But think of the shock Dewi had! Think how he feels!"

Mam nodded and reached out to stroke my head again. I was beginning to enjoy all this stroking .

"I've no idea what to do," she said, "But your Dad would. I'll have to tell him – right now."

"Whoa, hang on," said Lowri. "Not a good idea. We'd enough trouble trying to make you believe us. We'd need a miracle to persuade Dad. And anyway, Gareth is with him and we can't let him know what's going on."

"Why not?"

"Because Gareth just can't keep his mouth shut, can he? The story would be all around town and school in no time!"

"Oh gosh, no," said Mam, "but I still want to tell your father. He always knows what to do."

"Yes, he's great when we need to sort a drain or fix the car," said Lowri, "but I don't know how he'd handle this one."

"Well, we'll see," said Mam, "we'll wait for Gareth to go to bed and then tell him everything."

Lowri wasn't happy, but she agreed, and I nodded too. Dad's usually a pretty sorted, reasonable bloke, so I wasn't too worried.

Lowri climbed back into bed and I crawled back underneath in case Gareth walked in. Mam went downstairs to the kitchen to work out what exactly she was going to tell Dad.

CHAPTER 9

I MUST HAVE FALLEN asleep. I woke up because somebody was punching me in my stomach – my mother. She was talking so fast there were no commas.

"Dewi! I'm so sorry! I was so busy in the kitchen preparing my speech – and making a rhubarb tart to keep myself occupied while I was thinking – actually I made three – and a Victoria sponge. I had to do something because I was going mad! Then, because I was so busy, I didn't hear your Dad going to bed. I'd been popping my head round the door every now and then but they were both still watching some strange film, so he must have gone soon after Gareth – he did look tired come to think of it – and by the time I popped my head round again, he was long gone. I rushed to the bedroom and he was snoring away! I tried waking him but you know how he is!"

I did. Dad could stay sound asleep even if a JCB flew through the roof, and if anybody tried waking him before he'd had six hours in the

Land of Nod ... well, put it this way. I wouldn't try it.

"I tried shaking him and pinching him till he woke up but he was so rude! And he fell asleep again straight away so I've decided to leave it till the morning. OK?" I nodded. "Will you be alright here till then?" I nodded again. "You don't want to ... um ... go to the toilet or anything, do you?"

That's our Mam for you. Even in the middle of a crisis she was worried about the carpet. But as it happens, she was right, I was bursting. I nodded – a lot.

"Right," she said, trying to calm down and think straight, "I'll leave the doors open so you can just walk in and out yourself. I'm really exhausted now, but I don't know if I'll ever get to sleep with all this going round in my head. Lowri's fast asleep, bless her."

She was, too. Her father's daughter.

Mam started stroking my head again. "You'll be alright, Dewi. This won't last long now. Dad is bound to sort something out. Night night, son." She kissed me on my forehead, wiped her nose with a hanky and went downstairs to open the back door for me.

Poor Mam. I felt really bad for putting her through all this, but ... hey, it wasn't my fault I was all woolly!

I went downstairs and out through the door into the dark. But I could see just as well as if it was daylight. One, and only one good point of being a sheep. Well, and being able to run faster.

The sheep in the next field started bleating at me straight away; why did they have to be so rude? All nudge-nudge-wink-wink because of my growing horns. Huh. I walked past with my nose in the air. Then they started bleating that I was a snob. Sheep can be such morons.

I did what I'd been bursting to do by the gatepost, and then, as it was such a beautiful, clear night, decided to go for a walk. I crossed the road and followed the old cart track up towards the mountain. I felt like giving my legs a really good workout after being so cramped for so long under Lowri's bed. I started trotting, and before long I was by the pine forest halfway up the mountain. There's a high wall around the forest, higher than usual to make sure that no sheep get in. If any of them did manage to get in there, we'd never see them again.

I remembered Dad saying that there was a wild sheep in there somewhere; it had gone through a small hole as a lamb, and couldn't get back out – or didn't want to. He hadn't ever managed to find it. Even the dogs can't run too well under those low branches, and Dad had had to crawl along on his belly, Commando-style. After twenty minutes of being scratched to pieces all over his face and arms and being bitten to death by midges, he'd had enough. That was a few years ago, so that sheep would never have been shorn or docked or anything, so it probably looked really messy by now – if it was still alive. Odds were it had died after being infested by maggots because nobody had ever been able to dock its tail.

Anyway, the moon was full tonight and the mountains were black and silvery-gold against the dark blue sky. I could hear dozens of owls calling each other and a family of badgers playing by the river. Because I was an animal, none of them were bothered I was there and were all carrying on as normal, taking not a blind bit of notice of me. It was brilliant. Once again, I realised being a sheep wasn't all bad.

But suddenly, the adult badgers raised their snouts in the air and froze. Then all the night birds started screeching loudly at each other and flew away at speed. A weasel shot past me before disappearing down a hole in the roots of the beech tree behind me. I glanced back up to see that the badgers had gone too – within the space of a few seconds, every single one of them had scurried back down into their burrows. What was going on? I started feeling a bit nervous. Everywhere was dead quiet and it didn't feel right. I hurried back to the forest wall and hid behind a big rock.

I didn't hear a thing for ages. I was dying to lift my head to see what had scared everybody, but that would have been really stupid. I had pins and needles in my back legs and was aching to move a bit. I was just about to shift my weight carefully when I heard a rushing sound, the sound of something moving at speed but knocking into things, bleating in panic. It was the sound of something scared, really scared, running for its life. And it was coming from the forest – from the other side of the wall! I was scared now, no, I was terrified, and when I heard this 'something' trying to clamber over the wall opposite me, I thought I was going to die on the spot.

It was falling back down, screaming, howling, frantically trying to scramble back up, then throwing itself at the wall in a mad panic. Even though my brains were scrambled with fear, I realised I could understand some of what it was screaming. I could make out some of the words, but there were some other, completely foreign words in there. But basically, this poor creature was scared out of its wits and screaming for help.

I'm not sure what came over me, but I got to my feet and somehow managed to jump onto the wall. That's when I saw it: a massive, wild-looking ram trying frantically to scramble up from the other side. The terror in its eyes made my blood run cold. He managed to get his forelegs onto the top of the wall, and for a second, there was relief in his eyes. He was going to escape! He caught my eyes.

"Come on! You're almost there!" I bleated.

But before he could respond, his eyes froze and his face contorted with pain. Then he seemed to be focusing on something a long, long way away. Then he disappeared back down into the darkness with a scream.

Something had obviously got hold of him at the last minute and had pulled him back down. That's when I heard the most terrifying sound I've heard in my life. It was the roar of a wild animal, a big, blood thirsty, ravenous, furious animal from hell.

I'd never quite understood that saying about something being 'bloodcurdling' before. But I understood now. I leapt from the wall and ran for my life, just ran like hell without thinking where I was going, I didn't care where I went, I just wanted to get away from there, from that roaring. I jumped over streams and fences, ran through bogs and brambles, ran until my lungs were screaming and my legs were about to collapse. Then I fell. I went soaring over a ravine and landed in a river. But, thank God, it wasn't that deep and I managed to swim to other side. I lay down on the bank and started crying.

I must have fallen asleep or fainted, because when I opened my eyes, I didn't have a clue where I was. It was still dark and deathly silent. No sound of birds or animals of any kind, only the river rippling past and the wind whispering in the trees above me. I looked up towards the whispering, and that's when I saw a dark shadow silhouetted against the sky on the edge of the ravine. It was watching me. I could see the muscles on its shoulders gleaming silver in the moonlight and its cold, yellow eyes glinting at me. It was a panther. A black panther.

CHAPTER 10

THEY SAY THAT YOU see your life flashing before you just before you die, as if your brain jumps back into the past when it sees that your future's done for. All I can say is – it's true. I saw myself eating sheep droppings at the age of two; swigging from the pet lamb's bottle at the age of three; falling into the sheep dip as a big lad of twelve. I wanted to give my younger self a good kicking up the backside. If I hadn't done all that I wouldn't be in this situation now: a terrified sheep on a riverbank miles away from anywhere in the middle of the night – a sheep which was about to be ripped to bits by an enormous, ugly black cat with massive fangs and mean, yellow eyes.

It leapt over the ravine and landed gracefully right in front of me. It was purring. Well, more of a deep bass purring, the kind of sound a cat makes when it's faced with a plateful of finest raw steak. Lamb steak in this case. It curled its lips back to show its teeth. They were covered in blood and it obviously fancied a bit more blood for dessert.

"Please don't," I bleated pathetically as it got close, really close to my neck. "I'm not really a sheep! I'm Dewi – a thirteen-year-old boy who's too young to die!"

That was sheep-speak of course, and I knew a panther wasn't going to understand me, but it suddenly stopped in its tracks. It stared at me and slightly cocked its head to one side. Then it got really close again, sniffing me and staring right into my eyes. I stared back into its yellow eyes – and gasped. I knew those eyes, knew them really well.

"Menna? Menna Morgan? Is that you?"

The panther leapt back as if I'd stuck a needle in it. Its eyes didn't look half as scary now – in fact, they looked scared of me. It span round and jumped back up the ravine. It was one hell of a leap but, hey, it was a panther. It turned round once to look at me again then disappeared into the night.

I was in such a state of shock, I didn't notice for a while that I could hear birds and animals again. Owls were hooting above me and a weasel poked its head out of a hole right next to me. Then the dawns chorus started and I could see the first rays of sunrise in the sky above.

I got to my feet with a wobble and started

walking home. About half a mile from the road, I started turning back into myself again. Luckily, there wasn't much traffic around at that time of the morning. Somebody would almost definitely have had an accident if they'd seen a naked thirteen-year-old boy running across the road. A post van passed, but I jumped behind a wall just in time.

I managed to climb the stairs without making too much noise, had a quick wash in the sink and put on my pyjamas (and woolly hat) without waking Gareth. Then I climbed into bed and fell fast asleep straight away.

When I woke up, I was aching all over. I could hardly move. But I didn't have much choice. I ignored Gareth's protests and jumped into the shower before him. I had so many cuts and bruises, you could hardly see any bits of white flesh – and my horns had grown another two centimetres.

I tried hard to make sense of what had happened that night. That panther couldn't possibly have been Menna Morgan – could it? But it sort of made sense; it explained why she was so good at athletics – and why she was always grooming herself! If I could turn into a sheep, why shouldn't she turn into a cat? My imagination went nuts after that, and I started suspecting everybody of turning into some kind of animal at night. Could my mates be dogs and owls and mice and cockerels? No … that was a crazy idea. But then again …

I remembered the ram in the forest. Did I just dream all that? I dried my hair quickly with a towel, pulled my hat over my horns and rushed into the bedroom to get dressed.

"About time too! You were in there for ages!" said Gareth. "And since when have you started having showers before going to school, anyhow? Finally realised you stink? And what are those bruises?"

"Nothing. What time is it?"

"Quarter to eight. Why?"

"Just wondered." The bus wouldn't pass our stop until half eight, so I had time to get to the forest and back if I took the quad bike. I slid down stairs and grabbed my coat.

"Dewi!" squeaked Mam, as if she hadn't seen me for months. That's when I remembered I was a sheep the last time she saw me.

"Hi Mam! Sorry – no time to stop. Got to do something. See ya."

"But Dewi – your father!"

But I was gone. The bike was in the shed and the key was under the plastic Fison's bag. I turned the key in the ignition, kicked the bike into gear and off I went.

Fifteen minutes later, I was by the wall where I'd been trembling with fear – either in a dream or for real, I wasn't sure now – but my bruises were real enough. I switched off the engine and climbed the wall carefully. A few stones had come loose so it wasn't that safe. I swallowed hard and leant over the top.

There was hardly any of him left. Messy bits of wool, stained pink and brown; half a ribcage and a skull and other bits of bones scattered all over the place. Bits of flesh here and there, dried blood on the stones which the ram had pulled down as it tried to escape. The rest had seeped into a carpet of rust coloured pine needles.

Poor thing. He must have had a very lonely life in the forest with no other sheep for company. That's probably why he had such a strange way of speaking, he only had himself to talk to. It was a miracle he had lived so long, but to die like that … I climbed back down and stood there, shaking, for a while. So it had really happened; I could have been torn to pieces like that too. I could have been eaten – by Menna Morgan.

Would she be in school today? I had to see her. I jumped on the quad bike and roared back down the mountain. Dad was waiting for me by the shed.

"Where have you been?"

"By the pine forest. That wild ram's dead."

"What? You went looking for it just now?"

"Yes."

"Why?"

"Um … has Mam had a word with you this morning?"

"With me? Why should she?"

Oh, great. She obviously hadn't had a chance yet.

"Um … it's a long story, Dad. Can I talk to you after school?"

"What about? What have you done this time?!"

"Nothing! And I can't explain now, or I'll be late for school. Tonight, OK, Dad?"

But he didn't get a chance to answer because I'd shot into the kitchen. I managed to grab my bag and stuff a piece of toast with Marmite down my throat before running out of the door after Gareth and Lowri. Mam rushed out of the pantry.

"Dewi! He'd gone before I woke up, so I didn't get a —"

"Doesn't matter. Just seen him. We'll talk after school. Don't say anything till then 'cause he'll never believe you." She looked at me painfully.

"That's going to be hard. It'll be on my mind all day – I won't be able to think straight. I was awake all night worrying about you," she said, twisting her apron in her hands over and over again, hands that were rough and red after years of washing up, "and then I must have dropped off just before your Dad got up!"

"Don't worry, Mam, it'll be OK, honest."

I wasn't going to tell her about being within milliseconds of being eaten by a black panther, was I? I kissed her on the cheek – for the first time in years – and ran for the bus.

"Everything OK?" asked Lowri as we climbed on. But I didn't feel like telling her what had happened just yet, and anyway, somebody was bound to overhear us on the bus, so I just gave her a nod and sat with Bryn.

"How did you get on with the Geography homework?" he asked. Oh no … I'd forgotten all about it. It was supposed to be handed in that morning – or else.

I spent the rest of the journey copying Bryn's homework – changing a few words and figures here and there. Not all teachers are stupid – unfortunately.

CHAPTER 11

I CAUGHT MENNA MORGAN's eye for a second during assembly but she turned away immediately. I'm pretty sure she went red in the face too. We had French straight after Geography but there was no sign of her. She was obviously trying to avoid me because Ms Menna Perfect Pupil Morgan never, ever dodges lessons. So when break time came, I didn't play footie with the lads but went looking for her instead. I went round every block, inside and out, but there was no sign of her. With five minutes of break time to go, I saw her mates: Hanna Prys and Jenny Edwards. I walked towards them.

"Where's Menna?" I asked.

Chewing their gum like two old cows, they looked me up and down slowly, before staring at my woolly hat.

"What's it to you?" asked Jenny with a sneer.

"I just want to know where she is, OK?"

"Why? D'you fancy her?"

"What? Get lost! Just tell me where she is ... please."

They glanced at each other.

"Are we going to tell him?" Jenny asked Hanna.

"Dunno. Up to you," said Hanna.

They decided to keep on chewing, enjoying watching me get really worked up.

"Fine, forget it, the bell's going to go off any minute anyway," I said finally.

"Hold on," smiled Jenny, "she's on the athletics track. Practising or something."

"Thanks."

I ran down the path to the main road, shot through the Arriva buses car park, and flew past the hockey field towards the athletics track over the bridge. She was on her own, practising the hundred metres. She was doing pretty well too, until she saw me, then she stopped. I hurried towards her.

"Doing alright?"

"Yes. No thanks to you, scaring me like that."

"What? Are you scared of me?"

I caught her eye again for a second but she turned away sharply.

"As if."

"Menna ... it was you last night, wasn't it?" She bent to pick up her sweater off the floor.

"What are you on about? Last night?

Where?"

"You know as well as I do."

She was blushing, and she knew she was blushing.

"Look," I said, "we have to talk about this. I don't know why I turn into a sheep, but I want it to stop – and I'm pretty sure you'd like to stop being a cat too."

"A cat?! You turn into a sheep?! What is this? Some kind of sick joke?"

"No. Stop denying it, Menna, there's no point."

"Deny what?" she asked, starting to walk quickly down the track. "You have a problem, Dewi, but come to think of it, you've always been strange."

"Oh, come on, Menna! Give me a break! I'm asking for your help here, and I can help you too if you'll let me."

"I don't need any help from any one, thank you."

"Oh, and you'd have been quite happy to eat me last night, would you?"

She froze suddenly and stared at her feet. She didn't say anything for a while, then she turned and looked right into my eyes.

"Who knows?"

"What? That you're a panther? Only me." She

closed her eyes and breathed deeply. Hearing that was obviously a big relief.

"Promise me you'll never tell another soul about this, ever," she said, her yellow eyes burning into mine.

"I promise. If you promise me the same thing."

"Yes, fine. Promise. So what do you want to know?"

"How long have you been a panther and do you know why it happened in the first place?"

"Long story, and the bell's going to go any minute."

"Tough. This is more important."

So we sat down in the trees at the far end of the field where I told her my story and she told me hers. She'd started turning into a panther five years ago, and just like me, it always happened at night. But, unlike me, she never stayed in cat form longer every time, she was always herself again by sunrise. She had no idea why it was happening, even though she'd done loads of research. What worried her most was that at the beginning, she could restrict herself to catching and eating mice and moles, birds and their eggs and maybe a fox or two: wild animals that nobody would notice were missing. But lately, her panther self had been going for much bigger prey – like sheep,

"… and I'm scared I'm going to get shot any day now. Or I might even attack a farmer or a rambler or something."

"What? You mean you can't stop yourself?"

"Could you stop yourself from eating your mother's plants?"

"OK, no, I couldn't. But you stopped yourself last night didn't you?"

"Yes. But I recognised you. Usually, the panther part of me is much stronger. As a person, I don't want to hurt a mouse, let alone a sheep. The thought of it makes me feel sick, but when I'm a panther, I want – I need the taste of blood, I'm ravenous. Sometimes, I kill just for the sake of killing, for the thrill of it. And even though the part of me that's still me can't stand it, the panther part is just too strong. But when I recognised you last night, I was stronger."

"Phew. Lucky for me."

"Yes. But if I hadn't already killed that ram in the forest, I don't know what would have happened."

I felt a bit faint and started trembling when she said that. Menna didn't look too happy either.

"What are we going to do, Menna? We can't go on like this. And look, I've got horns that won't go away."

I took off my hat to show her.

"So that's why you've been wearing that horrible thing!"

"Well it wasn't a fashion statement, was it? Have you got something that won't go away?" She blushed, and nodded.

"Yes, but I can't show you."

"Why not?"

"Because it's embarrassing." I had no idea what it could be – until she pointed to her backside. A very nice backside, as it happens.

"What? Never! A tail?" She nodded again.

"A big black one. And it's getting longer and longer. I can strap it to my back at the moment, but it's getting harder and harder to hide. I can never go swimming with the others, and as for sunbathing ... well ..."

Thinking about her in a bikini with a big swishy tail was too much for me. I started giggling.

"Dewi! It's not funny!"

"No, I know it's not. But ... flipping heck, Menna, a tail? Sorry, but ...!" and I started howling with laughter. I laughed until the tears ran down my face. Then Menna slapped me – hard – right across my left cheek.

"Ouch! Hey! That hurt!"

"Good. It was meant to. Did I laugh when I saw your horns? No, I did not. And you look ridiculous. Put your hat back on."

"OK, but cool it, eh?" I said as I rammed my hat back over my ears and horns. "You can't hit a boy – I can't hit you back."

"You forget I'm half a panther. You're lucky I filed my nails this morning or you'd have no cheek left."

Fair comment.

"This is stupid," I said, "fighting like this when we should be trying to sort things out."

"You started it."

"Yes, I did and I'm sorry. Look, does your family know about this?"

"God, no! My Mam would have a fit! Why? Have you told anyone?"

"My little sister caught me out and we told my Mam last night."

"You never! How did she react?"

"She had a fit. And we're going to tell Dad tonight."

"And what will he do? Take you to the doctor's I bet, then the papers and the telly will hear about it and make your life hell and you'll be experimented on in a laboratory somewhere, just like ET!"

"Don't be so dramatic."

"And don't you be so naive. And don't you dare tell them about me! You promised, remember."

"Yes, but – "

"Look, if you tell them anything, I'll come over to your place tonight as a panther – and go without supper first ..."

"You wouldn't."

"Want a bet?"

I swallowed hard. I didn't want to bet a penny against those yellow eyes. I agreed on my mother's life that I wouldn't mention her at all, and that I'd tell her how Dad reacted in school the next morning.

Mam was waiting for us by the window when we came home from school.

"Gareth? It's about time you went to see your Nain."

"Uh? Me? Why?"

"Because she needs somebody to mow the lawn for her."

"Why me? Dewi can do it!"

"I've got another job lined up for Dewi. Now off you go, on your bike."

"My bike? But it's five miles away! Uphill!"

"It'll do you good. Hurry up, she's expecting you. And do a proper job of it, trim the borders and everything. She might give you a nice supper afterwards."

She only had to mention food, and Gareth's body language changed completely. He's such a gannet. As he disappeared up the road, Mam winked at me.

"Right, your father will be home for tea any minute. How are we going to tell him?"

"How are you going to tell me what?" said a deep voice behind us.

"Um … "

CHAPTER 12

MAM INSISTED ON FILLING the teapot and pouring everybody a cup of tea before saying a word. The bread and butter, jam, cheese and rhubarb tart were already on the table. Dad watched us all with knotted eyebrows, his eyes following Lowri carrying the milk jug from the fridge, Mam turning the teabags in the teapot with a teaspoon, and me sitting opposite him, trying to spread jam on a slice of bread and butter as if everything was perfectly normal.

"OK … what is it then? Have you dented the car again?" he asked Mam.

"Don't be silly."

"One of these two been sent home from school?"

"Course not," said Lowri.

"So why are you treating me as if I was sitting on a hand grenade, then? None of you can look me in the eye!"

He was right. But we kept on looking at our hands, feet and teapot.

Mam poured tea into four cups, passed them

round to us and sat in her usual spot next to Dad.

"Right," she said with a slight squeak. "We've got something to tell you, John. But before we do, you have to understand that it's not a joke, it's all true and very serious."

"Oh?"

"Dewi? It's your story ..."

Oh, no. Great, thanks a bunch, Mam. Everybody was looking at me now, but where was I supposed to start? And Dad was looking at me just like a headmaster, already convinced that I was guilty before even hearing an explanation.

"Well ..." I swallowed again, "it's like this, Dad. For almost a month now, something really strange has been happening to me at night."

"Oh?" He looked embarrassed for some reason.

"Yes ... I turn into a sheep."

There was a long, silent pause. Mam, Lowri and I were just staring at Dad and he was staring stupidly at me. Eventually:

"You turn into a sheep ..." he said slowly.

"Yes, every night. And then I turn back into me by morning, but I'm staying a sheep for longer and longer every time and I'm scared."

"Yes, of course, you would be," he said

slowly again. "And you're quite sure you're not dreaming?"

"No way. Lowri and Mam have seen me, haven't you?" They both nodded eagerly. "And … well … I've got these now, too."

I took off my woolly hat to show the horns that were already starting to curl slightly. If there was silence before, it was deathly now. Almost deafening. Dad stared at my horns, open mouthed. After a really long time, he got up and stood behind me. Then he grabbed my horns and pulled at them, really hard.

"Ooowww!"

"Sorry. Just wanted to make sure," he said, before sitting back in his chair with a thud.

"You do believe us, don't you Dad?" asked Lowri.

"Well yes, I have to …" he said. "It explains a few things, doesn't it? You ate all your mother's flowers, didn't you?"

"Yes, sorry, couldn't stop myself."

"Mm, yes, I remember."

Uh? That didn't make sense. What did he remember? Had he been watching me eat them or something?

He took a long sip of his tea, then sat up straight. "I'm glad you finally decided to tell me all this, but I should have worked it out from the very start." He coughed. "You see, there's something I've never told you." He placed his hand over Mam's and turned to her, "And I should have told you, of all people, but I thought it was all over, all in the past. But it obviously isn't. And I'm sorry." Then he turned to face me. "And I'm really sorry you had to go through all this, Dewi. I know from experience that it's not much fun."

Knew from experience? What was he on about?

"What are you on about, Dad?" asked Lowri.

"I went through exactly the same thing at his age. I was a sheep."

"What?" squeaked Mam.

"Really?" I whispered.

"Yes. And I was worried Gareth might turn into a sheep on his thirteenth birthday, but he didn't, did he? So I thought the curse had come to an end."

"Curse? What curse?" asked Mam, who had gone all red and purple in the face.

"My great-grandfather upset some gypsies years ago. He refused to let them camp on his land, accused them of killing and eating some of his sheep and sent them away with the help of his twelve-bore shotgun. One of the old women put a curse on him, saying that his sons and

91

the sons of his sons would turn into sheep. He didn't take a blind bit of notice – until Grandad started growing horns.

"Wow! Grandad had horns?!" asked Lowri, her eyes like dinner plates.

"Every night for years. Until he got married."

"John ... is that why you never took off your cap in front of me until we got married?" asked Mam, who'd gone a funny shade of grey by now.

"Yes. Exactly. Well, almost married. You remember that night after the local eisteddfod?"

Mam blushed immediately.

"John! Shush! That's enough."

"I don't get it," said Lowri. "The horns disappeared once you got married?"

"Yes, straight away."

"And that's what Dewi's going to have to do? Get married?"

"Yes, something like that," smiled Dad.

"But I'm too young to get married!" I said faintly, feeling slightly dizzy.

"And who'd have him anyway?" said Lowri.

Cheeky little cow.

"I don't think he'll have to get married," said Dad. "Dewi, come with me into the garden for a minute … Lowri, stay here with your mother."

On the wooden bench at the far end of the garden, Dad explained my options to me. No, I wouldn't have to get married, not in this day and age; the answer was much more straightforward. I was still a bit young for it though …

I was horrified.

"What? Sleep with a girl? Me? Dad! I can't!"

"No, I know that, and it's illegal anyway. So you'll either have to stay a sheep every night until you're old enough, or … there is another option, but it's practically impossible."

"What is it?"

He told me, and I felt dizzy again.

"Told you it was impossible, didn't I?" said Dad.

"Mmm …" I agreed. I was dying to tell him that it wasn't at all impossible, but I couldn't. I managed not to smile, and said:

"Look, Dad, you never know. So I'll go out tonight, alright? Just in case."

"But what's the point? It'll be like looking for a needle in a haystack!"

"Dad, we'll see, OK?"

I was on tenterhooks. I tried phoning Menna to tell her what had happened, but her mother said she wasn't home and was staying overnight at Jenny's. Really? She stayed over at a friend's house, even though she turned into a panther at night? Sounded a bit dangerous to me, but if she'd had five years of practice, she probably knew what she was doing. I didn't have her mobile number, so I tried phoning Jenny's house, but the line was engaged all the time. Her brother on the Internet, I bet. There's not a lot of broadband around here.

So I had no choice, I had to wait until it was dark. I could have waited another night and told Menna in the morning, but I didn't have the patience.

CHAPTER 13

THE SECOND I FELT my body beginning to change that night, I went out through the doors Mam had left open for me, and ran for the mountain. It was raining, the clouds were low and the wind was really strong. I was actually glad when I transformed completely – a sheep's fleece is better than any kagoul. Not that the rain bothered me that much; I had a panther to find. I wasn't worried about communicating with her. She had understood me the night before, hadn't she? OK, maybe what I had to say tonight was a bit more complicated, but she was bound to get the gist of it – as long as she'd had a good supper beforehand.

I wandered around for ages, bleating "Menna! Menna, where are you?" But there was no sign of her, only other sheep who thought I'd gone loopy and an annoying little weasel who kept following me around. It was pouring down now, and despite my thick fleece, I was cold and wet and fed up. And that's when I saw them – a bunch of men with guns. Trebor Davies, Wil

Hendre, and his brothers, Ned and Tom. Oh no … I went closer so that I could hear what they were saying. Ned Hendre was as fed up as I was.

"We won't see it tonight. Come on, let's go home, there's no point."

"And you'd be happy to see another dead sheep tomorrow morning, would you?" said Wil, his older brother. "One more hour, come on."

"But it might be just another stupid story! Just a cat that's a bit bigger than usual, you know what people are like," said Ned.

"I don't care if it's a cat or a dog or a mole with an AK 47," said Trebor, "something's ripping our sheep to bits, and I'll pump it full of lead if I see it. Come on. To that forest over there. That's where it was last night, according to John Bryn."

I froze. John Bryn ? That was my father! He must have gone to see the ram for himself and then told this lot. I came out in a cold sweat. Menna … they were going to shoot Menna!

I went round in circles for a while, desperately trying to decide what to do. But my brain was one big blob of candy floss and nothing made sense and none of my ideas went anywhere. I tell you, my sheep IQ was pretty low. In the end,

I ran round bleating "Menna! They're going to shoot you!" at the top of my voice. But in all that wind and rain, she would never hear me.

I could see the men climbing over a stile in the distance. I ran after them. But I didn't get further than the stile. I couldn't get up the damn thing! I tried at least a dozen times and almost broke my leg. Frustrated? You bet; I was cursing and swearing like no sheep had ever cursed or sworn before. In the end, I gave up on the stile and realised I'd have to go the long way round; through two rivers, a bog and a weak spot in the fence Dad had asked me to fix days before – thank God I hadn't got round to it.

I galloped off through the wind and rain. The first river was easy, but the rain had turned the second one into a raging torrent. It was all brown and furious with white bits on top. It looked dangerous. I walked along the bank for a while, until I got to a bit which looked more shallow. I stepped in carefully, and within seconds, I was swimming. Then I was underwater. Then I was on the surface again, spitting and retching and panicking. I'm quite a good swimmer, but I had no arms to do my nifty freestyle! No arms to grab the branches that were flying past my head!

Eventually, I hit a tree trunk which had

fallen across the river, and somehow, I managed to scramble up one of the branches and drag myself to the bank. I was half dead; it felt as if I'd swallowed most of the river and done twelve rounds with Joe Calzaghe. So I dropped down on the grass for a bit and tried to get my breath back. Then I remembered about Menna. I jumped to my feet again and ran as fast as I could towards the bog.

That was great fun in the rain. Imagine walking through a field of treacle in a pair of stilettos. That's what it feels like for a sheep. I was stuck in the bog for ages, bleating and sweating and swearing even more. But I made it in the end. I got back onto dry land (except that it was wet) and headed for the weak spot in the fence. I pushed myself through it – and got stuck again. The barbed wire had me well and truly hooked by the fleece. I tried reversing, but that only made things worse. So I pushed forward again, and got myself totally, completely stuck (I told you my brain wasn't that sharp when I was a sheep didn't I?). Brilliant. This was all I needed. And it was still bucketing down.

I could see the faint shadow of the forest in the distance and the men fighting their way towards it in the wind. I prayed that Menna wouldn't be daft enough to go to the same place twice. But if she was, and if she did, I could do nothing to help. I lay there, wanting to cry and wanting to kick my Great Grandfather up the backside for being so mean to those gypsies. If he'd let them camp in his field, I wouldn't be in this mess now, would I? If Trebor Davies and his mates killed Menna, I'd be a sheep for years, until I … well, you know what by now … but I'd be pretty upset about Menna too, of course.

Then I realised something was tickling the back of my neck. What the …?

"Don't move," said a squeaky little voice, "this is a very delicate operation." The weasel! That annoying little weasel was on the back of my neck! It must have followed me all the way.

"What the heck do you think you're doing?"

"Getting you out of this mess. The sooner you stop asking questions, the sooner I can get you free; I need to use my teeth to chew through your smelly wool, OK?"

"What? Oh, great, yes, brilliant, thanks. I'll shut up and let you …" Six seconds later, I just had to ask: "You didn't happen to see a black panther on your way here, did you?"

"Mffhhff." It had its mouth full. But it sounded like a 'No'.

I quite enjoyed the tickling sensation as the weasel tried gnawing through the tangled fleece; to be honest, I was enjoying it so much, I couldn't keep my eyes open. But they soon shot open again.

I felt it, more than I actually saw it. Something was out there in the mist, something big, something much bigger than me.

"Weasel?" I whispered.

"What now?!"

"Did you seem something pass just now?"

"All I can see is your wool. Now shut up."

"But weasel … there's something out there. Think you could hurry up a bit?"

"If you'd just stop interrupting me I'd have finished ages ago! Now shut your face!" I shut my face.

I stared out into the mist and rain. She was out there, I knew it. I couldn't see her, but I could feel her, her physical presence, her power, her compulsion for blood, for sinking her teeth into something with a pulse. Something like me. I was on a plate for her like this, like a piece of chicken on a skewer. I was a lamb kebab. I swallowed, but my throat was dry. The weasel was still frantically gnawing away, bless it, but half my fleece must have been wrapped around that barbed wire.

"Menna?" I whispered into the darkness, "I know it's you. Listen, there are two things you should know before you think of sinking your fangs into me."

The words sounded good – confident, even. But my voice didn't. I was trembling so much, my teeth were chattering.

"F-first point," I stuttered, "there are f-four blokes with guns just down there, looking for you. Second po-point, I know how we can p-put a stop to this once and for all." No response. No sound at all, nothing but the howling wind and spattering rain. "You are there, aren't you Menna? ... Menna?"

That's when I felt her breath next to my nose. Oh, no ... I could hear a low, but very clear snarling sound; it definitely wasn't a purr; it was a nasty, scary 'I'm going to kill you and shred you into tiny pieces' snarl. I heard the weasel squeak with terror and felt her slither off my back. Coward! But at least it had got me free at last – I could move, not that I dared move a muscle just yet.

"M... M... Menna!" I whispered, "Let's not rush this; think about it ... think seriously about what you're about to do."

More snarling, and her breath was so close, I could feel it on my eyeballs. I didn't dare turn my head, didn't dare blink.

"Didn't you hear what I just said? There are men with guns down there who will shoot you the second they see you."

I could hear her licking her lips. Oh, my God! "I know what's happened to us, Menna! Well, to me, anyway. It was a gypsy's curse. Honest! But I know how to stop it! We could do it here, now!"

The snarling stopped for a second and I turned my head slowly towards her. Boy, she was big. Her head was enormous, her teeth shiny and yellow and her eyes even more yellow; eyes that were still dying for a taste of blood. It looked as if she was going to bite my head off any second. I had no choice. I'd have to go for it that very second. So I did. I puckered my lips and kissed her. It wasn't just a prissy little kiss either, but a big, wet smackeroo, almost a full-blown snog. Not that it's easy for a sheep to snog anybody; the teeth get in the way. I kept my eyes open and could see the shock in her eyes, and then the anger. She was furious! Oh, oh … She pulled her head away and roared. No. Roaring was not a good idea. Not with twelve bores in the vicinity.

"Menna! That's how the curse is meant to be stopped! Give it a chance to work!"

But she was still roaring with rage, her fangs were dripping with saliva and she was opening her mouth even wider. I shut my eyes. And that's when everything shattered with an almighty crack – and I was in pain. Excruciating pain. So I was going to die after all, and I was only thirteen years old. I had managed, whilst still an animal, to kiss another person whilst they were an animal. That's what would shatter the curse for ever, according to Dad. But it hadn't worked.

I wanted to cry, but there was no point. I might as well take it like a man and die quietly. But gradually, I started realising that I was wet, very wet. I thought it must be the blood. But I was cold, and fresh blood shouldn't be cold. I opened my eyes. I looked down, and saw a pair of pink hands with fingers – human hands and fingers. I was myself again! And in one piece! I was alive! With not a spot of blood on me! I got to my feet – and yelled. I'd forgotten about the barbed wire. I crawled slowly out onto the field and looked around me. There was no sign of Menna, not as a panther nor as herself. There was no sign of Trebor Davies and his posse either.

"Hello?" I shouted. "Is anybody there?" Nothing. I was totally confused now. I'd heard a crack which had sounded just like a shotgun going off. Had they shot Menna? If so, where was she? And where were they? I ran around, shouting and yelling for ages, but I was freezing, almost hypothermic, so I gave up and set off for home. It was still very misty so I followed the stone wall down the side of the mountain. I was very, very worried about Menna, but what could I do? I decided to call out one more time, just in case.

"MENNA!!!"

"I'm here, no need to shout."

Huh? She was on the other side of the wall! I started climbing up.

"Menna! What are you …?"

"Don't you dare climb that wall!"

"Why? What's wrong?"

"I haven't got any clothes on, have I!"

"Oh, of course. Sorry. Neither have I."

"What happened?"

"I kissed you."

"I know that, you idiot! What happened afterwards?"

"No idea. I heard a crack or a bang, or something like a gunshot anyway, and I felt this excruciating pain, and then … nothing. Then I saw I was me again."

"That's exactly what happened to me. What

was the bang, then? Not the men with guns because I saw them going home ages ago."

"Oh. Well, it could have been the end of the curse. It sounded a bit 'final' didn't it?"

"It did. Well ... we'll see tonight, won't we?"

"Yeah. I expect we will." Silence. I was very conscious of the fact that I was naked. And that there was a naked girl on the other side of the wall.

"Right, I'm going to set off for home then, while it's still dark," said Menna.

"What, on foot? But your house is miles away!"

"I can hardly call a taxi, can I, you dipstick."

"Don't call me a dipstick! I've just managed to break the curse!"

"Yeah, well, we'll see."

"Boy, you're so grateful."

"Sorry. Look ... thanks for that," she said in a much kinder voice. "We can talk properly after school tomorrow – or today, I've no idea what time it is."

"Yeah, must be one or two in the morning. Right, see you, then."

"Can I ask you for just one more favour?" she asked.

"Yeah, what?"

"I'm going to go over this hill now. Will you

105

promise not to look?"

"Not to look at what?"

"Me, you dipstick! I don't want you looking at my bare bottom!"

I smiled.

"Of course I promise."

"Right. See you later, then. Unless we've both caught pneumonia."

I counted to five before climbing the wall carefully to look at her trotting up the hill.

Well? What would you have done?!

Ramboy is just one of a whole range of publications from Y Lolfa. For a full list of books currently in print, send now for your free copy of our new full-colour catalogue. Or simply surf into our website

www.ylolfa.com

for secure online ordering.

TALYBONT CEREDIGION CYMRU SY24 5AP
e-mail ylolfa@ylolfa.com
website www.ylolfa.com
phone (01970) 832 304
fax 832 782